# Disney
# Dragons, Mermaids, Fairies, and More

Random House 🏠 New York

rhcbooks.com

ISBN 978-0-7364-4244-2 (trade)

MANUFACTURED IN CHINA

10 9 8 7 6 5 4 3 2 1

# CONTENTS

# ℐNTRODUCTION

Since the beginning, Disney films have included creatures of different mythological or folkloric traditions as both friends and foes. From the fearsome or friendly dragon to the mischievous or motherly fairy to the daring or devious mermaid, these creatures have been vitally important to the storytelling in every film that has featured them. They drive the action, provide levity in dark situations, and help a main character discover their own special powers. In these pages, you can explore all the ways that mythology and folklore enter the Disney world to create unique and memorable characters that have captivated audiences for generations.

# The Blue Fairy

Kind and patient, the Blue Fairy gives Pinocchio life to reward Geppetto for his good deeds. She shows her displeasure when Pinocchio makes bad choices, but when he shows bravery and honor, she stays true to her promise to make him a real boy.

**Friends:** Geppetto, Pinocchio, Jiminy Cricket

**Foes:** none

**Home:** the stars

**Special skills:** magic

**Quote:**
*"Prove yourself brave, truthful, and unselfish, and someday you will be a real boy."*

# COREY THE MANTICORE

Once a mighty warrior, the Manticore—part lion, part scorpion, and part bat—now owns a popular family-friendly restaurant, the Manticore's Tavern. She's still up for a dangerous quest using her sword, the Curse Crusher, especially when someone she cares about is in trouble!

**Friends:** the Lightfoot family

**Foes:** the curse dragon

**Home:** the Manticore's Tavern

**Special skills:**
flight, breathing fire, strength, swordsmanship

## DID YOU KNOW?

The manticore myth started in Persia and was brought into European culture by a Greek physician in the 4th century BCE. In those early versions, the manticore did not have wings.

**Quote:**
*"You have to take risks in life to have an adventure."*

# Fairy Godmother

Optimistic and kind, Cinderella's fairy godmother brings a positive outlook to any situation. While she can be a bit forgetful, she is capable of amazing magic!

**Friends:** Cinderella, Gus, Jaq, Prince Charming

**Foes:** Lady Tremaine

**Habitat:** wherever she is needed most

**Special skills:** magic

**Quote:**
*"Bibbidi-bobbidi-boo!"*

# FLORA

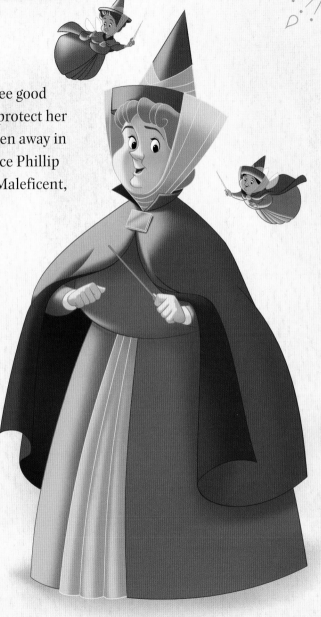

Flora, Fauna, and Merryweather, the three good fairies, took Princess Aurora in as a baby to protect her from the evil Maleficent and raised her hidden away in the woods. Skilled at magic, Flora arms Prince Phillip with the Sword of Truth to help him defeat Maleficent, who has transformed into a dragon.

**Friends:** Fauna, Merryweather, Aurora

**Foes:** Maleficent and her goons

**Home:** cottage in the woods

**Special skills:** magic, flight

**Favorite color:** red

**Quote:**
*"Thou Sword of Truth, fly swift and sure, That evil die and good endure!"*

## DID YOU KNOW?

The myth that inspired Aurora's fairy godmothers comes from English folklore, but it also has origins all over Europe.

# FAUNA

Fauna is sensitive and kind, but she's brave when it's time to defend Aurora. When Princess Aurora was born, Fauna gave her the gift of song.

**Friends:** Flora, Merryweather, Aurora

**Foes:** Maleficent and her goons

**Home:** cottage in the woods

**Special skills:** magic, flight

**Favorite color:** green

**Quote:**
*"I can only do good, dear, to bring joy and happiness."*

## DID YOU KNOW?

Unlike the fairies of Disney classic tales, folklore often features fairies acting against humans, using their magic to play pranks or cause illness.

# MERRYWEATHER

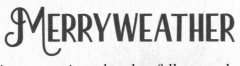

Bold Merryweather is more serious than her fellow good fairies. To help Aurora, she uses her magic to make the princess fall into a deep slumber, rather than die from Maleficient's curse.

**Friends:** Flora, Fauna, Aurora

**Foes:** Maleficent and her goons

**Home:** cottage in the woods

**Special skills:** magic, flight

**Favorite color:** blue

**Quote:**
*"And from this slumber
    you shall wake
when True Love's Kiss
    the spell shall break."*

# MALEFICENT

Maleficent, a dark and very powerful fairy, cursed King Stefan and Queen Leah's daughter, Aurora, after they neglected to invite her to Aurora's christening. Ever since, it has been Maleficent's goal to find the princess and get her revenge on the King, the Queen, and the good fairies.

**Friends:** her goons, her raven

**Foes:** Aurora, Prince Phillip, Flora, Fauna, Merryweather

**Home:** the Forbidden Mountain

**Special skills:** dark magic, teleportation, hypnosis, metamorphosis, curse inducement

## DID YOU KNOW?

Many cultures around the world have different versions of dragon myths. Maleficent's dragon form is based on a European version from the High Middle Ages.

**Quote:**
*"You poor simple fools, thinking you could defeat me. Me? The mistress of all evil?"*

# Pegasus

Created by Zeus as a gift for his newborn son, the heroic Pegasus soars through the sky as Hercules's loyal steed. While he takes his job very seriously, Pegasus can be playful and feisty when he and Hercules aren't busy fighting monsters.

**Friends:** Hercules, Phil

**Foes:** Hades, Meg (temporarily), monsters

**Habitat:** Mount Olympus (formerly), Ancient Greece

**Special skills:** flight

## DID YOU KNOW?

In Greek mythology, Pegasus is the offspring of Poseidon, the Olympian god of the seas, storms, earthquakes, and horses.

# Tinker Bell

Spunky and sassy, Tinker Bell is fiercely loyal to Peter Pan and the Lost Boys, and does her best to keep them safe. While her temper can cause her to make some rash decisions, she always does her best to solve any problem.

**Friends:** Peter Pan, the Lost Boys

**Foes:** Captain Hook, Mr. Smee

**Habitat:** Never Land, Pixie Hollow

**Special skills:** flight, using pixie dust

**Quote:**
*"I think I can fix that."*

### DID YOU KNOW?

Tinker Bell got her name because she is a tinker fairy, a fairy who mends things.

# The Mighty Manticore

Long ago, the world was full of amazing magic and fearless creatures on epic quests. One such creature was the legendary Manticore, who, with her trusty sword, could vanquish any threat to her land.

But eventually, convenient technology took over, making magic and quests a thing of the past. All of the formerly majestic creatures transitioned to more ordinary lives.

Many years later, the Manticore, better known as Corey, was no longer a fearsome beast. Her tavern, once filled with thrill-seeking adventurers, had become a family restaurant featuring a mascot, birthday parties, and karaoke.

One day, two young elves appeared in the tavern asking for the map to the Phoenix Gem, an ancient artifact of great power. She offered them a children's menu that was based on the map, refusing to give them the real thing. Quests are dangerous!

19

The elf named Ian pointed to a portrait on the wall. "Look at that Manticore. She looks like she lived to take risks!"

"Whoever said you have to take risks in life to have an adventure?" asked Corey.

"Apparently, you did," said Ian, glancing at the plaque above the portrait.

"You have to take risks in life
To have an adventure."
–the Manticore

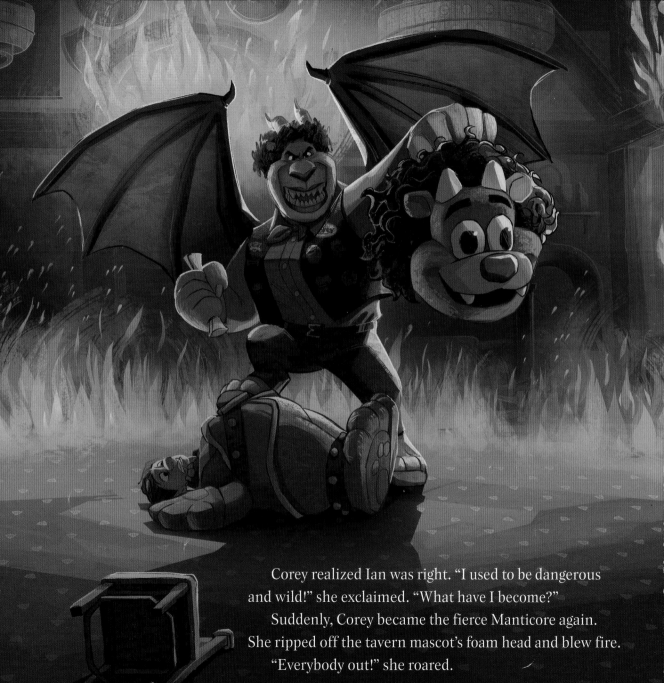

Corey realized Ian was right. "I used to be dangerous and wild!" she exclaimed. "What have I become?"

Suddenly, Corey became the fierce Manticore again. She ripped off the tavern mascot's foam head and blew fire. "Everybody out!" she roared.

Later that night, an elf named Laurel came to the tavern. She was the mother of the boys who had gone searching for the Phoenix Gem. The Manticore realized she hadn't told the adventurers there was a dangerous curse on the gem.

"All right—how do we help my boys?" asked Laurel as they drove away to find them.

The Manticore explained the Phoenix Gem curse to Laurel. "It's a Guardian Curse. If your boys take the gem, the curse will rise up and assume the form of a mighty beast."

Only her enchanted sword, the Curse Crusher, could defeat the beast. But she had sold the sword years before.

"Don't worry," she said, "I know just where to find it."

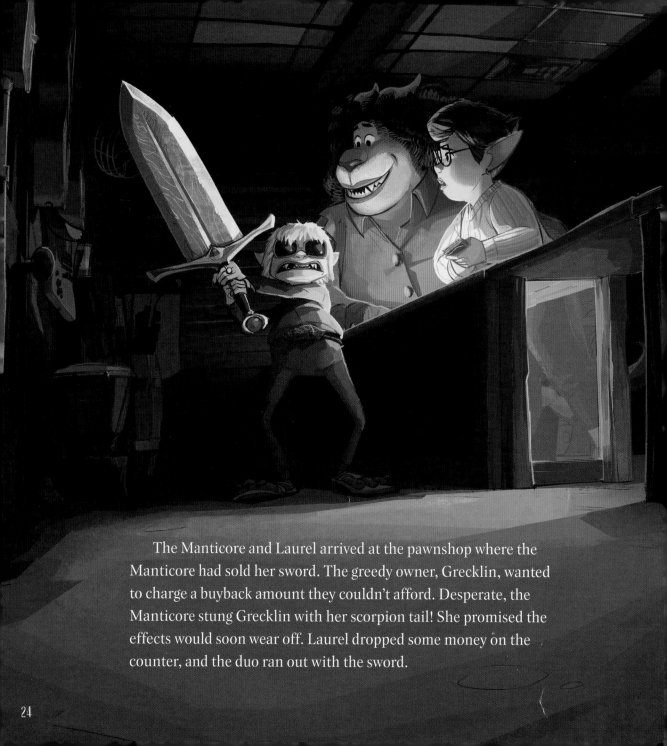

The Manticore and Laurel arrived at the pawnshop where the Manticore had sold her sword. The greedy owner, Grecklin, wanted to charge a buyback amount they couldn't afford. Desperate, the Manticore stung Grecklin with her scorpion tail! She promised the effects would soon wear off. Laurel dropped some money on the counter, and the duo ran out with the sword.

Back on the road, Laurel and the Manticore were racing to the boys when a sprite slammed into the windshield! Laurel swerved and landed in a ditch. Everyone was okay, but the car was a wreck.

Laurel watched the sprites fly away and turned to the Manticore. "How do you feel about exercising those wings?"

Laurel hopped onto the Manticore's back, and the pair quickly flew toward the boys. They found them . . . as well as the dragon from the curse! Wielding the Curse Crusher, the Manticore swooped down to help fight the fearsome beast. With both magic and strength, the group was able to defeat the dragon!

After defeating the curse dragon, Corey reopened her tavern, but this time, she vowed to stay true to her adventurous self. The Manticore was mighty once more!

# Barley Lightfoot

Barley is a fun, goofy elf who longs for a great and magical adventure! Those around him don't always take him seriously, but they know his heart of gold and optimistic outlook make him a great one to take along on any quest.

**Friends:** Ian, the Manticore, Blazey

**Foes:** Pixie Dusters, the curse dragon

**Home:** New Mushroomton

**Special skills:** extensive knowledge of Quests of Yore, driving his van, Guinevere

**Quote:**
*"Come, dear brother—our destiny awaits!"*

## DID YOU KNOW?

Elves originated in medieval Germanic mythology as creatures with magical powers and supernatural beauty.

Disney · PIXAR
ONWARD

# Ian Lightfoot

More serious than his brother, Ian is a wizard who inherited his dad's magic powers . . . but he has no idea how to use them. Ian wants more than anything to meet the father he never knew, and so when he finds out it is possible, he decides he'll face any fear to make it happen.

**Friends:** Barley, the Manticore, Blazey

**Foes:** the curse dragon

**Home:** New Mushroomton

**Special skills:** magic

**Quote:**
*"I think with a little bit of magic in your life, you can do almost anything."*

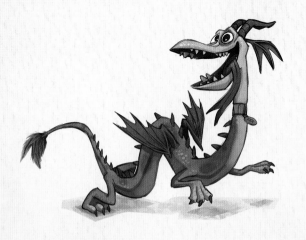

# Mushu

A tiny dragon with a big personality, Mushu joins Mulan on her quest in order to win back his position as a Fa Family Guardian. He really cares about Mulan, and goes to great lengths to help her save China.

**Friends:** Mulan, Cri-Kee, Fa Family Ancestors

**Foes:** the Hun Army

**Habitat:** China

**Special skills:** immortality

## DID YOU KNOW?

Mushu is a Chinese dragon. In Chinese mythology and folklore, dragons have many animal-like forms, but they are mostly depicted as snake-like. Imagine *Mulan* if Mushu had been shaped like a turtle!

**Quote:**
*"Hey! Dragon. **DRAGON**, not lizard. I don't do that tongue thing."*

# Philoctetes

Philoctetes, or Phil, is a satyr (half human, half goat) known for training the heroes of Ancient Greece. He has already retired when Hercules meets him, but he agrees to help the demigod because he thinks it's his chance to train the greatest hero of all time.

**Friends:** Hercules, Pegasus

**Foes:** Hades, Pain and Panic, Megara (formerly)

**Habitat:** his secluded island

**Special skills:** designing intense training obstacle courses

**Quote:** *"Giving up is for rookies."*

## DID YOU KNOW?

In Greek mythology, satyrs are male nature spirits, typically companions of the god Dionysus.

# Grand Pabbie

Wise and caring, Grand Pabbie is the leader of the Trolls and provides counsel to Anna and Elsa. While his guidance can be a bit cryptic, he is always trying to do what is best for his family, and for all of Arendelle.

**Friends:** Anna, Elsa, Kristoff, Sven, Bulda

**Foes:** none known

**Habitat:** Valley of the Living Rock

**Special skills:** magic, transforms into a rock, healing powers

## DID YOU KNOW?

Trolls are beings from Scandinavian folklore and Norse mythology. Like the trolls from *Frozen*, they are said to have lived in isolated rocks, mountains, or caves, but unlike the *Frozen* trolls, they were not known to help humans.

**Quote:**
*"Only an act of true love can thaw a frozen heart."*

# YETI

The Yeti, also known as the Abominable Snowman, is a monster who worked in the mail room at Monsters, Inc., before he was unfairly banished by Mr. Waternoose. Despite that, the Yeti enjoys his life in the human world.

**Friends:** Mike and Sulley, Bigfoot

**Foes:** Mr. Waternoose, Randall

**Home:** the Himalayas

**Special skills:** thick fur coat, a positive attitude

**Quote:**
*"Rule number one out here: Always . . . no. Never go out in a blizzard."*

## DID YOU KNOW?

The yeti comes from Himalayan folklore. The name roughly translates to "rocky bear," and it wasn't until the 1900s that European cultures adopted the myth and started calling it the abominable snowman.

# TROLL-SITTING

Anna, Kristoff, and Sven arrived in the Valley of the Living Rock as the sun was setting. The adult trolls needed to leave for a few hours, and the friends had volunteered to watch the troll tots! It was almost bedtime, so the group thought it would be an easy job.

But as soon as the adult trolls were gone, the babies started
running around! Anna and Kristoff tried to calm the little trolls, but
the harder they tried, the wilder the trolls became.

"Maybe they're hungry!" Anna said, heading for a basket of smashed berries. "Yummy!" she cooed. But the trolls clearly felt they had better things to do.

"Maybe they need changing." Kristoff bravely peered into one of the trolls' leaves. "Nope."

"Let's put them to bed," Anna suggested. "They must be tired by now."

But alas, the young trolls were wide awake.

Then something distracted the babies.
Their friend Olaf had arrived!

Anna and the little trolls ran to greet
Olaf. But in her hurry, Anna tripped and fell
face-first into the basket of berries!

Anna lifted her head. Her face was covered in dripping purple goop.

The little trolls burst into loud giggles. They stampeded toward her, lapping up the berry juice on her cheeks.

Anna laughed. "Well, I guess that's one way to feed them."

After the trolls were done, they sat in a heap, happy and full. Suddenly, a strange smell floated through the air. The trolls looked down at their leaves.

"Uh-oh," Kristoff said knowingly. "Olaf, you distract them."

Olaf happily told the little trolls a story. Anna and Sven collected new leaves while Kristoff changed the soiled ones. Soon everyone was clean and sweet-smelling once more.

"And now for my showstopping song about summer!" Olaf announced.

Anna noticed that the trolls were swaying. Some were having trouble keeping their eyes open.

"Actually," she said, "maybe Kristoff and Sven would like to sing a lullaby instead."

Kristoff grabbed his lute while Anna and Olaf put the trolls to bed.

"*Rock-a-bye troll-ys, in your small pen,*" Kristoff sang. "*Time to go sleepy for Uncle Sven.*"

By the time the adult trolls returned, the wee ones were sound asleep.

"Wow, great job," Bulda whispered.

"It was easy," Anna replied, elbowing Kristoff.

"Piece of mud pie," Kristoff added.

Bulda smiled and hugged her friends.

# Ariel

Curious, creative, and brave, Ariel is the youngest daughter of King Triton. She loves to explore the wreckage of old ships and learn about the human world, and longs to have legs and live on land.

**Friends:** Flounder, Sebastian, her sisters, Prince Eric

**Foes:** Ursula, Flotsam, Jetsam

**Habitat:** Atlantica

**Special skills:** beautiful singing voice, underwater breathing, fast swimming

**Quote:** *"Don't be such a guppy."*

## DID YOU KNOW?

The Little Mermaid is based on Hans Christian Andersen's fairy tale of the same name. But in that version, Ariel is more like an undine, a water nymph from German folklore.

# DAUGHTERS OF TRITON

ATTINA

AQUATA

ADELLA

ARISTA

ANDRINA

ALANA

# Hydra

Hydra is a sinister and deadly three-headed reptilian monster. Whenever one of his heads gets chopped off, another grows in its place. Hercules defeats Hydra on his quest to become a hero by causing a rockslide, protecting the city of Thebes.

**Friends:** Hades

**Foes:** Hercules, Phil, Pegasus

**Habitat:** Thebes

**Special skills:** regeneration, superstrength

## DID YOU KNOW?

Hydras come from Greek mythology, dating back as far as 700 BCE! Much like the movie, the original myth focuses on Hercules defeating the hydra, but in that version, Hercules's nephew Iolaus helps him.

# Luca

A friendly and curious sea monster, Luca lives under the water off the coast of a town called Portorosso, but he has always been interested in what happens there. When he meets Alberto and summons enough courage to explore life on land, he's thrilled to learn about all sorts of new things, from friends to pasta to school!

**Friends:** Alberto, Giulia

**Foes:** Ercole

**Habitat:** Ligurian Sea

**Special skills:** herding goatfish, bicycling

**Quote:**
*"I never go anywhere.
I just dream about it."*

# ALBERTO

Alberto is an adventurous sea monster who loves the land! He has a hideout, where he keeps all sorts of neat human things. He is happy to meet Luca and make a new friend, but when Luca becomes interested in things Alberto does not care about, Alberto feels left out.

**Friends:** Luca, Giulia

**Foes:** Ercole

**Habitat:** Ligurian Sea

**Special skills:** making and riding a scooter, eating pasta

**Quote:**

*"It's a human thing.
I'm kind of an expert."*

# Ursula

Power-hungry sea witch Ursula was banished from Atlantica long ago by King Triton. When she discovers Ariel's wish to live on land, she devises an evil revenge plot. Her ultimate goal is to become ruler of the entire ocean.

**Friends:** Flotsam and Jetsam

**Foes:** King Triton, Ariel

**Habitat:** her lair

**Special skills:** making magic potions, shape-shifting

**Quote:** *"Poor unfortunate souls!"*

## DID YOU KNOW?

The sea witch's design is based on an octopus, but Ursula has only six tentacles. Before deciding on this design, animators considered several different sea creatures, including manta rays and scorpion fish.

# THE PEARL OF WISDOM

It was the night before the Pearl of Wisdom ceremony. Ariel and her sisters were excited! On that special day, King Triton's daughters would each take on an official royal responsibility.

The day would begin when each princess selected a pearl from the palace's pearl room to mark the occasion. In the afternoon, there would be a ceremony to announce how each planned to help Atlantica.

Aquata wanted to teach music to young merpeople.

Attina was going to keep the coral reefs clean.

Adella looked forward to volunteering with elderly merpeople.

Ariel wasn't sure what she wanted to do yet.

In the pearl room the next morning, each princess found her favorite pearl. The royal jeweler hung the special gems on seaweed chains, which King Triton placed around his daughters' necks.

Before the ceremony, Ariel swam toward her grotto to think about how she could help the kingdom. Her collection always made her happy.

But on the way there, something caught on her seaweed chain and it broke, falling off Ariel's neck. The pearl started to sink.

"Oh, no!" Ariel cried.

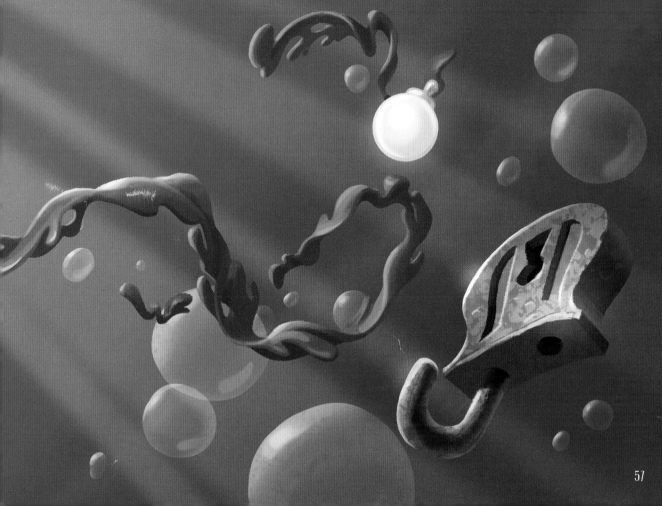

Ariel looked around frantically and saw that the
pearl had dropped behind an octopus. She raced
toward him, and he was so delighted to see the princess
that he waved at her with all eight of his arms—
accidentally flinging the pearl!

The pearl flew away and sank out of sight.

"Oh, Flounder," Ariel sighed. "I've lost the pearl! What am I going to do? How will I ever explain this?"

Suddenly, Sebastian appeared. "I've been looking for you everywhere," he cried. "The ceremony is starting!"

Ariel could not believe her eyes. There, behind his head, was her pearl! She quickly snatched the pearl and swam back to the palace.

Ariel arrived just as her last sister was finishing her announcement. "Tell us your promise, Ariel," King Triton said.

Ariel knew exactly what to say. "I am going to start a new museum dedicated to collecting and displaying beautiful sea art. And this pearl will be its first object."

The crowd cheered and applauded.

"You've made a wise choice, Ariel," King Triton said. "One that is in keeping with your generous nature. Today you and your sisters have shone brighter than any pearl ever could."

On the museum's opening day, Ariel couldn't have been
prouder to showcase some of the beauty she had found
under the sea!